over, under & through

and other spatial concepts
by tana hoban

aladdin books

macmillan publishing company   new york
collier macmillan publishers   london

Aladdin Books
Macmillan Publishing Company
866 Third Avenue, New York, NY 10022
Collier Macmillan Canada, Inc.

First Aladdin Books edition 1986

Printed in the United States of America

A hardcover edition of *Over, Under & Through* is available from Macmillan Publishing Company.

10 9 8 7 6 5 4 3 2 1

Library of Congress Cataloging-in-Publication Data
Hoban, Tana.
Over, under & through.
Summary: Photographs demonstrate the spatial concepts expressed in twelve words such as around, across, between, against, and behind.
1. Space perception—Pictorial works—Juvenile literature. [1. Space perception. 2. Vocabulary]
I. Title.
[BF469.H6 1987]   153.7'52   86-20675
ISBN 0-689-71111-5 (pbk.)

The photographs in this book were taken with two cameras: the Beseler Topcon RE Super D (35mm) with 58mm and 135mm lenses, and the Hasselblad 500C (2¼″ x 2¼″) with Planar 80mm f2.8 lens. The films used were Plus-X and Tri-X, developed in Ethol UFG and printed on Varigam paper in Dektol developer.

for miela and bob

over

under

through

on

in

around

across

between

beside

below

against

behind